The Lemonade Stand

by C.L. Reid

illustrated by Elena Aiello

D1481413

PICTURE WINDOW BOOKS

a capstone imprint

Published by Picture Window Books, an imprint of Capstone
1710 Roe Crest Drive, North Mankato, Minnesota 56003
capstonepub.com

Library of Congress Cataloging-in-Publication Data
Names: Reid, C. L., author. | Aiello, Elena (Illustrator), illustrator.
Title: The lemonade stand / by C.L. Reid ; illustrated by Elena Aiello.
Description: North Mankato, Minnesota : Picture Window Books,
[2022] | Series: Emma every day | Audience: Ages 5-7. | Audience:
Grades K-1. |
Summary: Best friends Izzie and Emma, who is deaf, open a lemonade
stand and learn how to run a business. Includes words in sign
language, a glossary, content-related questions, and writing prompts.
Identifiers: LCCN 2021006117 (print) | LCCN 2021006118 (ebook) |
ISBN 9781663909183 (hardcover) | ISBN 9781663921888 (paperback)
| ISBN 9781663909152 (pdf) Subjects: CYAC: Moneymaking projects-
-Fiction. | People with disabilities--Fiction. | Deaf--Fiction. | Best
friends--Fiction. | Friendship--Ficiton. Classification: LCC PZ7.1.R4544
Le 2022 (print) | LCC PZ7.1.R4544 (ebook) | DDC [E]--dc23
LC record available at https://lccn.loc.gov/2021006117
LC ebook record available at https://lccn.loc.gov/2021006118

Image Credits: Capstone: Daniel Griffo, 28 top left, 29 bottom,
Margeaux Lucas, 28 bottom left, Mick Reid, 29 top,
Randy Chewning, 28 bottom right, 28 top right

Design Elements: Shutterstock: achii, Mari C, Mika Besfamilnaya

Special thanks to Evelyn Keolian for her consulting work.

Designer: Tracy Davies

Printed and bound in the United States of America. PO4270

TABLE OF CONTENTS

MEET EMMA

EMMA CARTER
Age: 8 Grade: 3

SIBLING
one brother, Jaden
(12 years old)

PARENTS
David and Lucy

BEST FRIEND
Izzie Jackson

PET
a goldfish named Ruby

favorite color: **teal**
favorite food: **tacos**
favorite school subject: **writing**
favorite sport: **swimming**
hobbies: **reading, writing, biking, swimming**

FINGERSPELLING GUIDE

MANUAL ALPHABET

Aa Bb Cc Dd Ee

Ff Gg Hh Ii Jj

MANUAL NUMBERS

0 1 2 3

Emma is Deaf. She uses American Sign Language (ASL) to communicate with her family. She also uses a cochlear implant (CI) to help her hear some sounds.

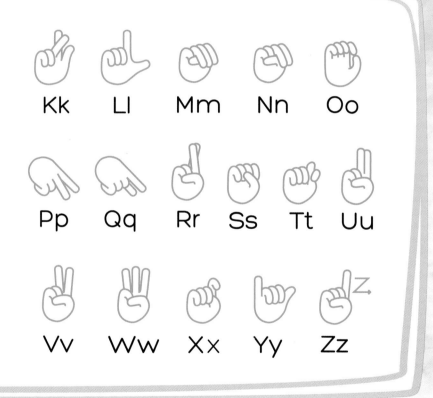

Kk Ll Mm Nn Oo

Pp Qq Rr Ss Tt Uu

Vv Ww Xx Yy Zz

4 5 6 7 8 9 10

Chapter 1

Business Planning

It was a hot summer day. Emma and her best friend, Izzie, were bored. They wanted something new to do.

"I have an idea! We can set up a
lemonade ✋✊✋✋✊✋👆✊
stand," Izzie signed.

"Great idea! We can be business
partners," Emma signed.

They smiled and shook hands.

"The front yard is the perfect
place to sell lemonade. Let's do it
every day for a week," Izzie signed.

"I am in. I want to buy my grandma a picture frame. I already have the perfect picture picked," Emma signed.

"Cool,"  Izzie fingerspelled. "There is a new graphic novel I want to buy."

"How much will one cup of lemonade cost?" Emma signed.

"I think one dollar is a good price," Izzie said. "I will make a poster tonight."

"And I have some balloons we can use to decorate our table," Emma signed.

"Let's start tomorrow morning at 11," Izzie signed.

"Deal," Emma signed.

They shook hands again.

Chapter 2

A Long Week

On Monday morning, Emma woke

up early. She put on her cochlear

implant (CI) just in time to hear

the doorbell.

"I am all set," she told Ruby, her

goldfish, as she rushed downstairs.

"Let's get to work!" Izzie signed.

Emma and Izzie made the lemonade. Then they carried a card table to the front yard.

They decorated the table and set up the cups. They grabbed their money box and were ready to go!

Business was good right away.

Jaden and his new friend were

the first customers. Jaden's friend

pointed at himself.

"Roberto," he said and fingerspelled to Emma.

"I have been teaching him ASL,"

Jaden said, smiling.

Jaden took a big gulp of lemonade.

"Yum,"  he fingerspelled.

After that, a big group of kids each bought a cup. A lady with a cute little dog bought two cups.

"This is fun!" Emma signed.

The next day was hot and humid.

Izzie accidentally knocked over the

pitcher of lemonade.

Sweet, sticky liquid spilled all

over the table! Several bees buzzed

around. One stung Izzie.

"Ow!" 🤛✌️ she cried.

Emma walked Izzie home. They didn't sell any lemonade that day.

It rained all day on Wednesday.

And on Thursday, they waited and

waited and waited, but nobody

stopped to buy lemonade.

"This is hard work," Emma

signed.

She was ready to quit. But she still needed more money to buy Grandma's present.

"Let's try one more day," Izzie signed. "And tomorrow, we will dress for success!"

Chapter 3
The Surprise

On Friday, Emma wore her teal

dress. It was her favorite. Izzie wore

her favorite outfit too.

And the weather was perfect!

"I have a surprise," Emma signed.

"What is it?" Izzie signed.

"Ta-da!"

Emma fingerspelled, uncovering a

plate of cookies.

"Cookies! That is a great business

idea!" Izzie said.

Not long after they opened for the day, a fire truck came by.

"Hi, girls! I'm Captain Olivia. We will take six cups of lemonade, please," she said.

After the firefighters left, people just kept coming. Emma and Izzie even had some repeat customers from earlier in the week.

By the end of the afternoon,

the girls were out of lemonade and

cookies. They were out of energy too.

"Being in business is hard work,"

Emma signed.

"But it was worth it," Izzie

signed, shaking the money box.

"We are two smart cookies,"

Emma signed.

"We sure are!" Izzie signed back,

laughing.

LEARN TO SIGN

bored

Twist finger at side of nose.

cup

Make C shape and bring hand to palm.

thirsty

Point to chin and move finger down throat.

cookie

Rotate C shape.

money

Bring back side
of hand to palm.

buy

Move top hand away
from palm.

summer

Bend finger while sliding
across forehead.

thank you

Move hand away
from lips.

GLOSSARY

business—work or a job

cochlear implant (also called CI)—a device that helps someone who is Deaf to hear; it is worn on the head just above the ear

customer—a person who buys goods or services

deaf—being unable to hear

energy—the strength to do active things

fingerspell—to make letters with your hands to spell out words; often used for names of people and places

humid—damp or moist

sign language—a language in which hand gestures, along with facial expressions and body movements, are used to communicate

TALK ABOUT IT

1. If you could open a business, what would it be? Why?

2. Emma adds cookies to their business. Do you think that was a good decision? What else could the girls have done to get more customers?

3. Use the fingerspelling guide at the beginning of the book to sign three words. Have a friend guess the words.

WRITE ABOUT IT

1. Pretend you are Emma. Write a letter to your grandma telling her about your lemonade stand.

2. Make a list of at least five things you could do when you feel bored.

3. Emma and Izzie make good business partners. Write a few sentences about a person you would like to work with.

Ruby

ABOUT THE AUTHOR

Deaf-blind since childhood, C.L. Reid received a cochlear implant (CI) as an adult to help her hear, and she uses American Sign Language (ASL) to communicate. She and her husband have three sons. Their middle son is also deaf-blind. C.L. earned a master's degree in writing for children and young adults at Hamline University in St. Paul, Minnesota. She lives in Minnesota with her husband, two of their sons, and their cats.

ABOUT THE ILLUSTRATOR

Elena Aiello is an illustrator and character designer. After graduating as a marketing specialist, she decided to study art direction and CGI. Doing so, she discovered a passion for illustration and conceptual art. She works as a freelancer for various magazines and publishers. Elena loves video games and sushi. She lives with her husband and her little pug, Gordon, in Milan, Italy.

5